The Car

by Lily Browne
illustrated by Edward Crosby

Harcourt
SCHOOL PUBLISHERS

Printed in China

ISBN 10: 0-15-350632-6
ISBN 13: 978-0-15-350632-1

Ordering Options
ISBN 10: 0-15-350598-2 (Grade 1 On-Level Collection)
ISBN 13: 978-0-15-350598-0 (Grade 1 On-Level Collection)
ISBN 10: 0-15-357798-3 (package of 5)
ISBN 13: 978-0-15-357798-7 (package of 5)

4 5 6 7 8 9 10   0940   15 14 13 12 11 10 09

Kevin, Maggie, and I liked it when we went camping. Mom and Dad let us help put up the tent. First, I took away the sticks and stones from the ground. Then Maggie pulled the tent out of its bag and started to open it up.

"Put the tent poles together first," said Maggie.

Snap, snap, snap! Kevin and I
snapped the tent poles together. We
put the poles inside the tent, and the
tent grew taller.

Then we pushed the pegs in the ground and lifted the loops over the pegs. The tent was strong. It would not blow over. The rain would not get in.

4

Dad came toward us. He was carrying our sleeping bags. I put them in the tent and made up our beds. Our tent looked like a welcoming place to sleep at night.

Mom put a mat down at the edge of the tent. "This mat will help keep our tent clean," she said.

Dad and Maggie started building
a fire. A boy from the next tent came
to help, too. His name was Nate. He
asked us to come and play by his tent.

6

"Good!" said Mom. "All the hard jobs are done. Tomorrow, I'll feel more like I am having a rest."

"All the hard jobs *are* done," I said.
"Can I go play with Nate by his tent?"

"Stay where we can see you," said
Mom. "When you smell food over the
fire, you will know that it's time to eat!"

8